I0845774

# The Complaint Department

# Chapter 1 The Complaint Department

Solomon Greaves never asked for this job.
He wasn't looking for it, didn't pray for it, and certainly never imagined himself as the middleman between the creator and the weary world below.

When the Creator first appeared to him, it wasn't with a grand trumpet or a holy choir, not even a whisper wrapped in thunder. It arrived as a simple sentence in the dark, somewhere between sleep and waking:

*"If you're so sure I'm not listening, then listen for Me."*

That was it. No flashes of light. No burning bush or glowing staircase. No contract written in cloud ink. Just… an appointment. Silent. Inevitable.

And so, Solomon Greaves — once a tired schoolteacher whose voice had carried over restless classrooms, found himself named the Creator's first and only Complaints Officer.

His task? To gather grievances — divine, human, systemic, personal — and do what no celestial being had done in millennia:

Listen.

At first, he thought it was a cosmic joke. He told his friends over coffee. They laughed until their mugs trembled. He told his church. They prayed for his sanity in hushed, worried tones. He tried sharing it online. He was promptly unfollowed, muted, and politely blocked.

Solomon Greaves faced a daunting challenge: convincing the world that his appointment was genuine. He knew that merely claiming to be the Creators' first official Complaints Officer would invite skepticism, mockery, or worse. And yet, the task was his.

His first attempt was subtle. Solomon stood in public squares and places of worship, sharing the story of his encounter with the Creator. His words fell on deaf ears. Few listened, and those who did assumed he was yet another eccentric chasing visions.

Still, the words in the dark had taken root, and Solomon — stubborn as unpolished stone — pressed forward.

When mouths would not open and ears would not bend, he turned instead to walls. If people would not hold the story, then brick and timber would. The message, he decided, needed a home before it could find a crowd.

The office building began as a skeleton of repurposed brick and stubborn faith, assembled at the crossroads of two tired streets The mortar still smelled faintly of dust and rain, as if the building itself had been listening for years before he arrived. Around it, the streets carried the weary pulse of a place that had once tried to dream itself into prosperity— one lined with cracked sidewalks, fading shop signs, and the ghosts of small ambitions. On the north side, an old tailor's shop leaned into its own shadow, its window still displaying a mannequin in a half-finished suit from another decade. Across the way stood a diner that had changed hands too many times to count, its neon sign sputtering through the fog of early mornings.

Before it became an office, the building had lived a dozen other lives—first as a grain exchange in the 1920s, then a print shop, then a small church that met only on Sundays until the congregation vanished. For a brief, forgettable stretch, it housed a pawn shop, its walls lined with the lost promises of the town's residents: watches, wedding rings, and guitars that never found their way home. Now, with its windows scrubbed clean and its bricks breathing again, the building seemed to wait—like the town itself—for something worth believing in. Above the door, Solomon hung a small wooden sign:

# THE COMPLAINT DEPARTMENT

At first, no one came with anything real. People wandered in for the novelty — to ask if he took customer service complaints or if Creator offered refunds. Some rolled their eyes, some took selfies, and most left without filing a single word.

Passersby paused and took photos. Some posed beneath the sign with exaggerated frowns, pretending to file fake grievances. Others shook their heads and muttered, "Another one gone strange."

After the third week of jokes — and one too many carvings of "kick me" scratched into the wood — Solomon painted over the sign with gold leaf and re-hung it. Below the decree, he added a second inscription:

**WE LISTEN. WE DON'T JUDGE. WE CAN'T FIX, BUT WE WON'T LOOK AWAY.**

This caught the attention of one elderly man who had never smiled since his wife died. He read the new line and sat quietly on the steps. He didn't speak, not at first. Just sat. And after several hours, when Solomon finally opened the door and asked if he needed anything, the man whispered, "I just needed someone to see me."

Solomon realized then that the jokes didn't matter. The laughter, the graffiti, the ridicule — none of it mattered as long as even one person found comfort. And just like that,

Solomon took his first official complaint. He listened to the elderly man for hours that day. Giving no advice, no solutions. Simply bearing witness to the complaint and affirming the elderly man's existence by hearing and acknowledging his words, his thoughts his grievances.

Solomon went through the ritual he had designed for hearing, recording and filing complaints. He first asked the client for their permission. Then, as he listened, he recorded the conversation. He then placed the recording in an envelope stamped with the time, date the person's name , and their thumbprint  on the envelope and filed it in the appropriate filing drawer. As this was his first complaint; he created the first drawer's name plate " invisible". For clients that did not wish to be recorded , Solomon would just request a simple hand written note with their complaint written on it. They could sign it or leave it anonymous. It made no difference as long as they were heard.

After the elderly man's visit, the Complaint Department was quiet again. The waiting room stayed empty. The desk stayed bare. And the silence became heavy.
He could not bear the stillness. It felt less like peace and more like erasure — as if the world had already forgotten what it had heard.
Words alone had failed. So, Solomon took action to solidify the Creator's words. He reached for something more permanent.

The first time Solomon carved into stone, he bled. Not the noble blood of heroes — just the raw, stinging scrape of skin meeting grit, the kind that seeps slow and stubborn. The work was awkward, each strike of the chisel clumsy, ringing too sharply in the cold morning air.

The granite slab he dragged from the quarry was far too heavy for one man. He'd inched it along the road over the course of two days, pausing only when his back screamed or when the weight of it pressed the air from his lungs. People stopped to watch — not to help, only to marvel at the strangeness.

He could have ordered a plaque. Stone, he thought, would stay. Quiet. The kind that refused to flinch when mocked. If the people would not believe his words, perhaps they would believe the permanence of carved truth.

The slab stood nearly as tall as he was, veined with iron and streaked with age, its skin cool even under sunlight. The surface was uneven, roughly smoothed by days of effort. Each cut of the chisel bit into him as much as into the stone.

When it was done, the words stood in shallow, unsteady grooves:

**By decree of the Creator, this Department exists**


**to hear the unspoken griefs of humankind.**


**All complaints shall be received.**


**None shall be ignored.**


**Silence shall not win.**

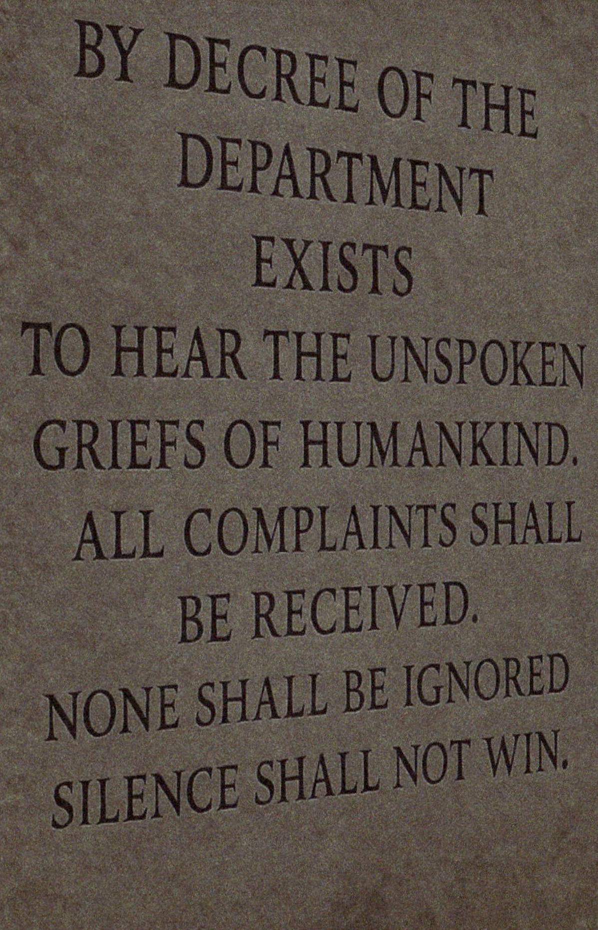
BY DECREE OF THE
DEPARTMENT
EXISTS
TO HEAR THE UNSPOKEN
GRIEFS OF HUMANKIND.
ALL COMPLAINTS SHALL
BE RECEIVED.
NONE SHALL BE IGNORED
SILENCE SHALL NOT WIN.

No author's name. No flourish. No plea for belief.
Only the facts as he had received them — stripped of
ornament, because truth should not need decoration.

People came to look. Some admired the craftsmanship with
quiet curiosity. Some snorted. One teenage boy — too
restless to leave anything untouched — spray-painted
*CREATOR'S YELP REVIEW* in jagged black letters
beneath the inscription before running off, his laughter
echoing down the block.

And still… no one filed anything.

Each morning, at exactly 7:00 AM, Solomon unlocked the
Complaint Department's door as instructed — though no
reason had ever been given for the hour. The ritual was as
plain as the room itself.

The desk was unvarnished wood, edges softened by age.
The chairs were mismatched — one with a cushion worn
thin, the others rescued from thrift stores and donation
piles. On the desk, a small tray held sharpened pencils and
stacks of fresh paper cut into neat rectangles.

For weeks, the tray remained untouched.

The waiting became its own shape — not quite failure, not
quite patience.
Sometimes he wondered if the silence itself was a kind of
submission.
Maybe the people had run out of hope that anyone, human
or divine, could hear them.

At night, he walked the same circular route through town,
letting the rhythm of his steps press down the questions.
Past the bronze statue in the park, whose arm had been

broken off years ago. Past the rusting water tower whose paint flaked like old memories. Past the alley where teenagers lit fireworks, each spark a brief rebellion against the curfew.

He started hearing complaints in the wind, in the edges of conversations that weren't meant for him. In the strained voice of a man arguing into his phone. In the brittle pause before a woman said *never mind* and walked away.

He wrote them down — unsigned, unclaimed — and filed them himself.

**Complaint #27:** *My wife died before we had our first real vacation. I can't stop picturing the hotel brochure on our fridge. It's still there.*

**Complaint #41:** *My daughter changed her name and cut off contact. I keep sending birthday cards. I don't know if she reads them.*

**Complaint #56:** *I was kind, and I was still crushed.*

**Complaint #58:** *I buried the truth so well that even I forgot where I put it.*

Each night, he slid the slips into a drawer labeled in small, deliberate letters:
**UNCLAIMED GRIEF**

Every morning, he reopened it — just in case someone came looking for their own. But the drawer stayed full, as if grief preferred the safety of being unnamed.

One afternoon, restless, Solomon stepped outside and stood beside the slab again. The letters were already weathering, chipped by wind, scratched by fingernails, worn by disregard. He placed his palm against the cool surface, feeling the faint tremor of the chisel marks beneath his skin.

"Why won't they come?" he whispered.

A child passing by slowed, squinting at him. "Are you talking to the rock?"

Solomon smiled faintly. "Not today," he said. "Today I'm just listening to the silence."

And the silence, though it had no words, felt heavier than stone.

So, Solomon stopped waiting. He took the Department to them.

He walked to homes split by silence, where conversations had long gone brittle.
He stood in market squares where neighbors shouted across crates of mangoes and oranges, each trying to drown the other out. He slipped into courthouse benches and prison cafeterias, where air was thick with stories no one wanted to write down.

He came without sermons, without solutions. Only with  a small recorder, a scuffed leather notebook and a pen that rarely left his hand. He didn't argue. He didn't promise. He just… listened. Slowly, the murmurs began.

"That man with the strange job," they said. "He sat with me after my mother died. Didn't try to fix anything. Just sat there. And somehow… I felt seen." He came without invitation. Without flyers or websites or loud proclamations.

Within a year, the Complaint Department was full. Not with filing cabinets or forms, but with people.
They came from across the city, across borders, carrying grief in invisible envelopes. Some brought rage like smoldering coals. Others brought disappointment so sharp it cut their sentences in half.

And Solomon, in his gray coat with the soft eyes, received every single one. But deep down, the question gnawed at him. Why him? Why had the Creator chosen a widowed schoolteacher with no training in conflict resolution, no experience in celestial administration, and a heart that had long ago stopped believing in miracles? And what, exactly, had he complained about that night — the night when the stars blinked strangely, the air held its breath, and The Creator replied?

# THE COMPLAINT DEPARTMENT

Solomon Greaves grew the Complaint Department into a sanctuary for learning and growth.

Cornplaints were heard to foster understanding.

Leaders, teachers, and healers trained others in empathy and resolution.

# Chapter 2 Into the Noise

Solomon's mistake — if it could be called that — was believing complaints would come neatly written on paper, signed in ink, filed under tidy headings.
He had imagined order: carefully chosen words, quiet voices, a civilized exchange between grievance and record.

But silence… silence grows teeth. It gnaws at the edges of patience until it becomes its own kind of noise — the kind that burrows under the skin, louder with every hour.

One morning, as if being led by an unseen force. Solomon rose from his chair, locked the front door of the Complaint Department, and walked straight into the world's noise. The first house he visited was too quiet. Not the gentle quiet of peace, but the tight, breathless quiet of people holding in more than they could say.

Through the thin curtains, he saw a couple sitting at opposite ends of a dining table. The food between them steamed faintly, untouched. Their hands rested on the table, palms down, like anchors.

He knocked. After a pause, they opened the door.  Solomon presented , No title. No sign. No preamble.
"I believe you have a complaint," Solomon said, "but you don't know how to say it."

The husband's brow furrowed. The wife's eyes widened.

And then — as if the air had given her permission — the woman began to cry.
Her shoulders shook. She covered her mouth as though even her grief was an inconvenience.

Solomon stepped inside, pulling out a chair to sit between them.
He didn't ask for backstory.
He didn't try to fix their marriage or their dinner.
He simply listened until the sobs turned into words, and the words into something quieter still.

Next came the marketplace.

The  market smell of overripe fruit, dust, and the faint rot of things held too long. Stalls leaned at awkward angles, their tables crowded with bruised apples, wilting greens, and the sweet rot of split figs.

Two men stood nose to nose, shouting over a crate of spoiled pears. Their hands twitched at their sides — the fight was looking for an excuse.

Solomon stepped between them.
"Are you angry about the fruit," he asked, "or something else entirely?"

The men froze, baffled by the question.

Finally, one admitted, "My brother just died. I don't know how to be around people anymore."
The other man blinked once, slowly. His jaw slackened.
"My brother died last month. I know the pain," he said, softer this time.

Someone in the crowd whispered, "I lost my brother too."
And for a moment the whole marketplace felt like a wound trying to close.

The fruit stayed on the ground. They walked away without it.

Word began to follow him, though never as an announcement — more like a shadow.

He became a whisper passed in waiting rooms and bread lines.
The man in the gray coat.
The one who doesn't judge.
The one who asks the question under the question.

He appeared in places people avoided unless forced: eviction hearings where the air smelled faintly of mildew and loss; hospital lobbies where every cough seemed too loud; addiction clinics where hope wore thin at the elbows; courthouse hallways that echoed with heels, boots, and the restless shuffle of chains.

To each person, he asked the same thing:
"What haven't you been allowed to say?" he asked.

And when they answered — halting, furious, or afraid — he told them,
"Your complaint is valid. Even if no one ever told you it was."

Not everyone welcomed him. Mercy rarely arrives on schedule.

A businessman shoved him out of an elevator, muttering about lunatics.
A pastor accused him of blasphemy and threatened to have him barred from the church steps.
A woman, standing outside a shuttered school, hurled cold coffee in his face.

But Solomon did not stop.

He understood now: complaints rarely arrive in tidy form. They live in muttered curses, in illnesses that deepen when no one listens, in bitterness disguised as a joke at someone else's expense.

Each night, he returned to the Complaint Department and began filing away the day's complaints.

He filed into drawers labeled **INVISIBLE, UNCLAIMED GRIEF** and **SUPPRESSED FURY.**

The labels engraved in deliberate capital letters:


Some entries read:

**Complaint #102:** *My mother told me to smile while my uncle touched me.*
**Complaint #119:** *I was fired for being too outspoken, then replaced by someone who sounded just like me.*
**Complaint #124:** *They told me to pray more. My depression did not listen.*

One evening, Solomon found someone waiting for him in the complaint department's lobby.

She sat in the lone chair by the window; her hands folded around a worn photograph. A child smiled from the image — two front teeth missing, eyes older than they should have been.

He sat beside her.
"What's your complaint?" he asked softly.

Her voice was almost steady. "I forgave too much. She whispered. I let them stay. I called it love."

She handed him the photograph.

Solomon didn't reach for his pen.
Some griefs are too sacred to be turned into paper and ink.

He simply held the photo for a moment, then gave it back. And for the first time that day, the Complaint Department was completely silent —not  the silence that gnaw, but the kind that bears witness. And in that moment, he understood: The Department was not the building it was him. Wherever he walked, it walked.

And as the day dimmed, Solomon realized he had entered the world's noise not to calm it, but to hear what it had never been allowed to say.

# Chapter 3 The Forgotten Altar

Before there was a Complaint Department, before the first form was ever filed, there was her. The woman who could turn a barren room into a warm home with nothing but her presence. Her illness had taken years from her, but she had given those same years back to him with tenderness.

The woman whose laugh felt like sunlight even on the coldest morning. And the woman who, in the last years, carried her suffering like a secret flame — small enough to hide, and hot enough to burn.

The sickness had been with her so long it became part of the  furniture of their days.
A shadow in the corner.
A weight in her voice.
The quiet inhale before pain made itself known.

Solomon learned the patterns of her struggle the way some men learn the tides —
when the fever would rise, when the light would hurt her eyes, when she needed to sit in the stillness just to breathe.

They spoke often in those days, but rarely about the thing waiting between them.
She would ask about the market, the neighbors, the way the old fig tree bent in the wind.
She would ask him to read  a book aloud, even if he stumbled over the words.
And sometimes, when she felt strong enough, she would take his hand and guide it to her heart, as though reminding him: *I'm Still here. Still us.*

On the last night, the room was lit only by a single candle. The air smelled faintly of rain and the herbs she liked to keep under her pillow.

Her breathing was shallow, but her eyes were clear. "Solomon," she said, her voice softer than the flame's flicker.
"I have spoken to Him."

She didn't mean the village priest.
She didn't mean a messenger.
She meant the One she believed had been with her since birth.
Her Creator.

"What did you say?" he asked, afraid to hear and unable not to.

She smiled faintly — the smile of a woman who has already crossed a threshold but is willing to linger a moment longer. "I told Him about my life. My joy. My sorrow. The years I waited for children that never came. I told Him about you — that you were my gift, my miracle in a world that gave me little else.

And yes… I told Him I wished I had more time with you." She paused, as though listening to something Solomon could not hear. "But then… I asked Him to release me. The pain has been a long road, and I am ready for its end."

Solomon wanted to protest, to bargain, to promise that things could still get better. But she lifted her hand — not to hush him, but to steady him.

"I also asked Him to watch over you when I am gone. To make sure you do not close your heart. To make sure

AND YES... I TOLD HIM I WISHED I HAD MORE TIME WITH YOU.
BUT THEN... I ASKED HIM TO RELEASE ME. THE PAIN HAS BEEN A LONG ROAD, AND I AM READY FOR ITS END.

you do not sit in silence when you could be enjoying the world." Her fingers tightened on his. "Promise me, Solomon. Share your grief, anger, and loneliness. Even when it hurts. Especially then."

Solomon whispered his promise.

And in the quiet that followed, she exhaled one final time not in defeat, but in release.
It was not a sound of defeat, but of release — like a bird let out of a cage, rising into a sky without end. The candle burned down to its base. The rain stopped. And Solomon sat there until the room was cold, holding the hand that had once held his whole future.

He carried her words with him into every conversation, every listening, every day that came after. They would be the unseen beginning of the work he had yet to start.

What he did next determined his current situation. When he remembers it now, it seemed like a dream but not.

To remember how he got to the alter Solomon had to remember his beautiful wife's death. The way he felt the overwhelming despair of that night when he began his walk to nowhere.

Solomon Greaves was just a man with a desperate prayer. Before he was the Creator's Complaints Officer, he was simply a husband unraveling.

It was a night soaked in grief —
not the kind that storms through with wailing,
but the kind that seeps in quietly
 and settles in your bones like damp that refuses to dry.

His wife had died not in an instant, but by slow surrender
— one prayerless day at a time.

The illness had arrived like a question no one wanted to
ask.
The doctors gave their answers in sterile tones, speaking in
measured sentences that left no room for miracles.
The church sent casseroles — hot at first, then lukewarm
with each passing week, until even pity went stale.
None of it helped.

That night, the night of his wife's last breath. Solomon did
not call 911, he did not cover her body, he did not call
friends, or family. Solomon simply wept for hours . He
wandered barefoot into the woods behind their home, not
knowing where he was going, only that he could no longer
stay. The ground was cold, uneven, uncaring beneath his
feet. His fingers clutched a broken photo frame; its glass
fractured into spiderweb lines that distorted the last picture
they had taken together.
He wasn't searching for anything. He was simply walking
away from the place where everything had ended.

The forest seemed endless in the dark, each tree leaning in,
branches whispering secrets to each other. Somewhere, an
owl called once and then fell silent. The air smelled of rain
that had not yet fallen.

It was there — in that labyrinth of shadow and damp —
that he found the altar. The altar seemed to breathe, as
though waiting for someone to remember it.

It was a ruin more than a monument: a crumbling stone
outpost half-swallowed by ivy, its corners blurred by moss,
the carvings on its surface worn to ghosts of shapes. It

looked as though time had meant to erase it but hadn't
gotten around to finishing the job.

Solomon's current memory is that he stood before it,
breathing hard, staring at the cold, unyielding stone.
Something in him cracked. He didn't remember shouting.
He was sure that he whispered.

However, he remembered his voice was hoarse as he asked
his questions.

"Why must the kind be tested until they break?"
"Why build a world where love is punished?"
"Why must we suffer? " "

He remembered shouting " Why does no one listen!"

And then
For the first time in his life
Something answered

The wind stilled.
The leaves froze mid-rustle.
Even his grief paused to listen.

The air thickened until it felt almost visible — heavy
enough to rest on his shoulders. He did not know if he fell
to his knees or if the ground simply rose to meet him.

And then a voice came — not from above, not from within,
but from beyond.
It spoke with the unhurried certainty of something that had
always existed:

**"If you're so sure I'm not listening then you listen"**

**"You shall be My Complaint Officer"**

**" All complaints shall be received.**

**"You shall take all complaints from 0800 until"**

**"You shall hear the unspoken griefs of humankind."**

**"None shall be ignored."**

**"Silence shall not win.'**

There was no celestial fanfare. No burning light. No great unveiling of heaven.
Just that voice.
And the unbearable weight of realizing it was not a metaphor.

He did not remember whether she appeared before the voice, or after—only that she was always near when something broke.

He buried that night for years, deeper than memory, deeper than fear. He filed it away in the part of the mind where you store things you're afraid will undo you. He replaced it with the daily rituals of survival: sharpened pencils, neat stacks of paper, drawers full of grief that wasn't his.

But now — standing in the Complaint Department Day after day — the memory had returned. Not as a gentle reminder, but like thunder rolling backward across the sky.

BUT SOMETHING STILL NAGGED AT ME DEEP DOWN. I NELT AND REFLECTED ON MY ORIGINAL COMPLAINT...

I HAD ONCE CRIED OUT: WHY IS LIFE SO UNFAIR?

WHY DO WE SUFFER WITHOUT REASON?

WHY DO GOOD PEOPLE PERISH?

WHY MUST THE WORLD BE SO CRUEL?

One evening, after locking the Department early, Solomon walked the old path back into the woods. The air was colder than he remembered, and the trees had grown denser, taller — like sentinels watching his approach.

The altar was still there. Time had not spared it. The moss was thicker, the cracks deeper. Small plants had rooted in its crevices. Yet it stood, stubborn in its ruin.

Solomon knelt. The soil was damp beneath his knees. He placed both palms on the stone. His fingers trembled, but his heart was steady.

"I remember now," he whispered.
"I came here because I was tired of being ignored."

The wind shifted.
The air changed — the same charged stillness as before.
And for the second time in his life, the Creator spoke:

**"You are still being heard."**

The tears that came now were not the sharp, burning kind. These were tired, holy tears — the kind that fall when truth arrives, not as relief, but as clarity.

After listening to all the creator had to say he understood:
He had not been chosen to fix the world.
He had been chosen because he had asked the only question that mattered.

**Why does no one listen?**

He stayed there until the sky deepened to black, and the stars scattered themselves across it like a slow, deliberate offering.

When he returned to the Complaint Department, he did not
feel lighter — but he felt anchored.

He walked to the drawer labeled **UNCLAIMED GRIEF**,
slid it open, and placed a fresh slip inside:

Complaint #0:
**Why does no one listen?**

His first question.
Humanity's oldest wound.

# Chapter 4 Heaven's Terms

The Creator did not give Solomon a speech that night.
There was no golden scroll unrolling from the clouds.
No shimmering signature from angels, penned in light.

Only his — words delivered with the weight of stone
dropping into still water:

**"If you believe the world is unjust…
then receive its sorrow."**

**"If you believe I do not listen…
then listen in My place."**

**"If you believe there must be change…
then become the vessel, not the fire."**

Solomon had always assumed divine callings came with
glory — maybe even a little power. The kind of authority
that made kings bow and enemies' scatter.
He never expected… filing cabinets.
Endless grief.
The hollow ache of listening to thousands of cries he could
not fix.

This was the contract.
Not written in ink, but in exhaustion.
No solutions.
No miracles.
Only the assignment to sit in the storm — to keep his eyes
open when every instinct begged him to look away.

By the fifth year, Solomon understood he could not do it
alone. For the first time since the altar, he wondered
whether listening might truly be enough.

He began to train others. Not priests wrapped in doctrine.
Not prophets hungry for visions.
Listeners.

They were teachers who had learned to hear the pain
between a student's words.
Artists who had spent decades giving shape to unspeakable
feelings.
Retired nurses who still remembered the trembling of hands
they could not save.
Formerly incarcerated men and women who knew the
sound of regret from the inside out.
Immigrants who carried the weight of two countries in their
chests.
He welcomed them all.

They came.
They learned.
And often, they wept — for the grievances they heard, and
for the ones they remembered from their own lives.

The Complaint Department grew.
It was no longer just a place to file sorrows; it became a
sanctuary for what the world had discarded. Not just
grievances — but people.

For a time, it worked.

The air in the town shifted.
Council meetings ended without shouting.
The marketplace saw fewer fistfights.

Overdoses slowed.
There were even weeks when the funerals stopped.

People laughed again inside the Department's walls.
They brought music, someone brought  an old guitar
missing two strings, another brought a half-tuned piano
whose remaining strings still vibrated  when coaxed.

They told stories.
Elders arrived to unload decades of silence.
Children wandered in with small complaints about unfair
chores, bad dreams, or the color of the sky.
Solomon accepted every filing without judgment, whether
it was drenched in tears or drawn in crayon.

The momentary global joy seemed as if it would last but, it
did not. Hate returned. But this time, it wore new clothes. It
began with a video.

A lecture Solomon had given — about listening without
conditions — was sliced into jagged fragments, the tone
stripped of context, captions bent to mockery.
His calm face appeared beneath bold text:

*"He wants us to hug racists."*
*"He says murderers deserve to be heard."*
*"This fool believes empathy will save us."*

It spread like fire on dry grass.
The internet moved quickly.
So did the cynics.

Soon, the Complaint Department began receiving
grievances about Solomon himself. He read the grievances
against himself without defense, but not without ache.

One read:
**"Complaint #111408: This man doesn't live in the real world."**
Another:
**"Complaint #111409: My pain deserves vengeance, not paperwork."**
And another:
**"Complaint #111410: Listening won't stop the bombs."**

Solomon did not defend himself.
He had learned that defense often sounds like dismissal to those already wounded.

The human spirit was caught in a global spell  part hate, part desperate faith and everyone was fighting to claim the world's belief.

Instead, he opened a third drawer.
He labeled it with careful handwriting:

**Weaponized Disillusionment.**

Because the world had grown too tired to believe in healing. But then something happened that had never happened before.

An unlabeled drawer opened — by itself.

It was the middle of the night. Solomon had fallen asleep at his desk, the glow of a single lamp haloing his face. The air was still, heavy with the scent of old paper and cooled tea.

The metallic creak startled him awake.
He watched as the drawer slid out on its own.
Inside was a single envelope. Unmarked. Its edges seemed to pulse faintly, as if holding back light.

He picked it up. The paper was warm against his fingertips. He opened it carefully.

Inside was a short note, written in a hand he had never seen before.

**COMPLAINT #000:**
*Humanity has ignored My warnings.*
*Division deepens. Cruelty spreads.*
*Final notice.*

*Signed,*
**The Creator**

The envelope slid from his fingers and landed on the desk. The room darkened — not with shadow, but with something heavier, like mourning made tangible. The silence that followed was not peace. It was the sound of a door closing somewhere far away.

The Creator had filed a complaint. And it carried an ultimatum.

He didn't sleep that night. The creator's complaint remained on the desk like a wound refusing to close. Morning came, but brought no relief. The sky outside the Complaint Department was pale and uncertain, as if it too was waiting for something.

It was the next evening, just as Solomon sat down again — unsure whether to pray or prepare for the end — that the door creaked open.

She entered without knocking, her presence as familiar now as it was unsettling. The woman in the Gray Shawl had returned.

:CREAK

COMPLAINT #000:
Humanity has ignored
My warnings.
Division deepens.
Cruelty spreads.
Final notice.
Signed.
The Creator.

# Chapter 5 The Gray Shawl

She didn't knock.
She never did.

The door simply opened, as if the air itself had granted her passage, and she stepped inside with the quiet certainty of someone who had been here before — and knew she would come again.

Solomon recognized her instantly.
The lines on her face were unclaimed by time, as though age had tried and failed to leave its mark. Her eyes were the real giveaway — dark pools, holding too many lifetimes to belong to any one soul.

Not death.
Nor fate.
But something adjacent— an emissary of endings.
A herald of the moment before a break.

She always came before something fractured beyond repair. The first time, she appeared the night his wife's chest rose for the last time and did not fall again.
The second time, when the Creator's voice first found him at the forgotten altar. The third, just before the floodwaters licked the stone steps of his childhood church.

And now — here she was again. After each of her appearances, he remembered a little more and a little less. As if she took some memories with her and left others behind like breadcrumbs. Or perhaps he was losing his grip entirely, and neither she nor the Creator existed outside his unraveling mind.

She wore a Gray Shawl draped over her shoulders; the wool frayed at the edges as if it had been brushed by centuries. Her half-smile was full of grim knowing, the kind you only wear when you've seen the same ending arrive in a hundred different disguises. Solomon felt the room shrink around her presence, as though even the air understood she was not a visitor but a verdict.

She sat without invitation in the chair across from him, legs crossed, hands folded in her lap like a woman politely waiting for tea she already knew wouldn't come.

"So," she said, her voice carrying the low timbre of inevitability, "you've made it this far. I'll admit — I didn't think you'd last."

Solomon did not answer. Silence was easier  and safer than giving her the satisfaction of being right.

"He filed a complaint, didn't He?" she asked, her tone as casual as if she were asking about the weather.

Solomon nodded once. Pretending would have been pointless — she always seemed to know the truth before he spoke it.

"And you opened it?"

"Of course."

"Then you know," she whispered, leaning in slightly, "your kind has failed."

The words landed heavy, like stones dropped into deep water. Solomon wanted to argue — to summon a defense,

to name the lives changed, the small mercies saved — but
all he could see were the drawers full of evidence against
him.

The memes.
The venomous videos.
The way compassion had been twisted into comedy.
The students who left his training burning with resolve,
only to be smothered by the cold machinery of inherited
hate.

He had done good.
But good was no longer enough.

"There's still time," he said, though the words came out
softer than he intended — meant more for himself than for
her.

Her gaze didn't waver. "Is there? The wars have already
begun in whispers. The next filing you'll receive won't be
words, Solomon. It'll be blood."

She stood, brushing invisible dust from her skirt, as though
the conversation was already concluded.

"You were never meant to win," she said, her voice almost
tender now. "Just to prove how far they could fall — even
with help."

His fists tightened. "That's not the Creator's way."

She paused at the door, turning just enough for him to see
the shadow of a sad smile.

"You think we and the Creator agree on everything?"

Then she was gone — leaving the door slightly ajar, as if endings preferred to keep a way back in.

Solomon sat in the silence she left behind, his breath shallow, his thoughts circling.

He opened a new drawer in the cabinet.
He wrote in clean, deliberate script:

**Pre-War Whispers**

And instantly a complaint appeared in the drawer

**Complaint #111900: Even hope can be mocked until it dies.** Signed by **Gray Shawl.**

Solomon nodded with understanding.

Outside, somewhere far from the quiet safety of the Complaint Department, a ripple began.

Across countries.
Across refugee camps and market stalls.
Through cracked political screens, between playground fights, into parliaments already simmering with fire.

The whisper became wind.
The wind became shouting.
The shouting… became action.

Solomon rose from his chair, walked to the switch, and turned off the lights. The darkness folded around him like a shroud. He knew what was next.

She always arrived when something in him — or the world — was about to break.

# Chapter 6  Memories of The Lady

Solomon Greaves remembered her long before he ever knew to fear her. The woman in the Gray Shawl did not announce herself. She simply *arrived*. She had no title, no scent, no name that lingered in the mouth. Only memory— and even that faded around her like smoke in the wind. But Solomon remembered the eyes. They were never angry. They were never warm. They were… evaluating.

She came before things broke. Not a broken as in bad or good just a break, a change. That much he understood.

**The First Visit: The Last Breath**

The night his wife's chest rose for the last time and did not fall again, the woman appeared in Solomon's home, her shawl soaked from the rain but her presence completely dry.

He hadn't heard a knock. He'd simply looked up and there she was, seated in the corner of the kitchen where the lamp didn't quite reach. The air shifted when she entered, as though the room recognized her before he did.

Solomon was weeping. Not wailing — weeping. The silent kind of sobbing that only love and inevitability can coax from the ribs. His wife had whispered goodbye moments earlier, her lips barely brushing the air.

"She was stronger than you," the woman said, voice soft as wool yet piercing as a blade.

He hadn't answered.

"She loved you as you are. That's the cruelest kind of love. It leaves you defenseless."

He gripped the table.

"Will you weep forever, Solomon? Or will you rage?"

That night, she showed him a truth. Not in visions or spells, but with words. She placed an image in his mind like a video memory of where to go. An altar — ancient, crumbled, forgotten in the hills hidden places. "If your grief is as righteous as you think, perhaps He will listen. But grief alone doesn't move Him. Anger might."

When she vanished, the air settled — but the chair beside him remained warm, as if she had never truly left., he hadn't seen her feet move. Just the door opening, then closing behind a shape that should not have known the house.

And so, Solomon followed the video in his head, his feet stumbling along the path. He couldn't stop himself from walking . He was compelled to arrive at the altar.

**The Second Visit: The Creator's Voice**

Solomon had screamed at the heavens. He'd cursed fate, time, and all the brittle injustices of the world. He screamed until his throat bled. Solomon, then asked his fated question. And when his voice fell to silence, another rose from beyond. The words were felt within him and around him.

**"If you're so sure I'm not listening then you listen"**

**"If you believe the world is unjust…
then receive its sorrow."**

**"If you believe I do not listen…
then listen in My place."**

**"If you believe there must be change…
then become the vessel, not the fire."**

Solomon collapsed.

And from the shadows of the ruined altar's archway, the woman stepped forward again.

"So," she whispered, "the Creator speaks."

She paced the ruins slowly, her finger trailing along broken stone. "And just like that, you're converted? No questions? No suspicion?"

"I know what I heard," Solomon rasped.

"Or what you *needed* to hear."

He stared at her.

She smiled—not with her mouth, but with her presence. "Tell me, if the Creator has finally appointed a Complaints Officer, is that a promotion or a punishment?"

Solomon didn't answer. He had no answer.

"I'll be watching," she said, and disappeared into wind that did not move.

**The Third Visit: The Rising Flood**

Months later, after his encounter with the creator, Solomon went to his childhood church. He had wanted to share his experience at the alter with those who once taught him to sing hymns and recite proverbs.

But they laughed.

One called him a blasphemer. Another accused him of pride. None of them believed. Even the pastor turned away.

While Solomon spent hours trying to convince them a thunderstorm rolled in with howling winds. By midday it was unsafe to leave by nightfall, they were trapped.

Solomon stayed, not out of loyalty — but guilt. As thunder cracked and water climbed the stained-glass windows, he went outside to the front steps, seeking help.

That's when he saw her again.

She stood on the surface of the floodwaters, dry as bone. Rain parted around her. Wind fled from her Gray Shawl.

"You've chosen the wrong audience," she said.

"They're good people," Solomon replied.

"They're terrified people. They mocked you until they needed you. That is not belief — that is bargaining."

"What do I do?"

"You walk alone. That is your calling. Not to seek love. Not to seek praise. Just to *listen*."

She paused. "Speak less. Hear more. That's how complaints become understanding. That's how noise becomes change."

And then she was gone.

The waters never reached the chapel's front door — they never could. The church sat atop more than twenty stone steps. No one died that night. But they remembered the night of the storm.

And so did he.

She came before fracture. She never explained why. He wished he could ask her why she came. He wished he could ask her what she wanted.

But questions were offerings, and he had none left to give.

But Solomon began to understand that she was not a herald of doom—she was a *mirror*. She did not cause pain. She revealed what must be faced. And she made certain he never forgot who he was, what he was asked to do, and why it would never be easy.

# Chapter 7 The Collapse

The whisper became wind.
The wind became shouting.
And the shouting… became fire. Explosions, death.

It began with fractures — hairline cracks in the shell of the world that widened before anyone could brace for the break. The world wasn't breaking; it was remembering every crack it had ignored.

A protest in a coastal city turned deadly.
A treaty, years in the making, unraveled in a midnight tweet.

A border dispute reignited an old resentment like dry grass catching a single spark. The world was at war again. This time it was to prove once and for all who the creator's chosen ones were.

Whose belief system came with the strongest branding and the most ruthless marketing. Whose belief in the creator was so great that they were obviously the chosen ones. The ranking of beliefs was the new social status.

You had to verify your belief structure to gain and maintain, housing, work , food, and the right to marry. Every word said or  even thought was parsed by AI.  Your belief was monitored by an algorithm that believed in nothing. No facts were needed just a strong belief in whatever group ruled your land.

From his desk, Solomon watched the headlines scroll like obituaries:

**"Tensions Escalate."**
**"Talks Fail."**
**"Missiles Launched."**

And though the words burned on the screen, he felt something colder seep in: the quiet, private question he never dared to voice aloud —

*Had the Creator truly spoken to him… or had he been speaking to himself all along?*

He remembered the first night, years ago, at the ancient alter when the voice had come — not from the alter, not from the clouds, but from somewhere inside his own ribs and beyond. There had been no proof. No witnesses, unless she counted. Had the woman in the Gray Shawl been there before the voice… or after? If only, he could be his own certainty.

But certainty, he had learned, could erode under enough doubt.
And lately, the tide was coming in.

Still, he did not panic. He filed.

**Complaint #1115529:** *My daughter is now a soldier. Her birthday is next week.*
**Complaint #1115541:** *I didn't know my neighbor was from 'the other side' until they told me I had to choose a side.*
**Complaint #1115554:** *I stopped praying. Not because I lost faith, but because I didn't know what to ask for anymore.*

The sky turned red in the north, not like sunset — but like a warning the earth itself was trying to speak.
Sirens replaced birdsong.

Social feeds didn't go quiet because people stopped posting — they went dark because everyone was screaming at once.

The Complaint Department became a shelter.
Cots lined the hallways.
Tea brewed in repurposed plastic buckets, poured into mismatched mugs.
Volunteers came in waves — some former cynics, others longtime believers.

Children made signs in bright crayons and broken grammar. **"PLEASE FILE PEACE."** Solomon took their complaint and added it to the others.

The war of belief was raging, death was everywhere. Solomon moved through it all like a ghost — present, but only in outline.

He hadn't slept in days. His hands shook when he wrote. The lines of his own handwriting wavered, curling into a language only fatigue could read.

But he kept filing.
Because even if the world was ending, someone still had to listen.
Even if *He* had never spoken.
Even if the voice at the alter had only been his own mind begging him to try.

One morning, the room hummed again — the same way it had the night everything began. An envelope appeared on his desk. Hand-delivered. No stamp.

Inside, it read:

**Complaint # 11119902:** *You did your best. It still wasn't enough.*
*Signed: Anonymous*

He set it down without flinching.
Sometimes the cruelest complaints were the ones you silently agreed with. He felt the weight of every grievance he had ever filed pressing back against his ribs.

In the distance, bombs fell.
Nearer still, hearts broke. And yet…

The whisper became wind.
The wind became fire.


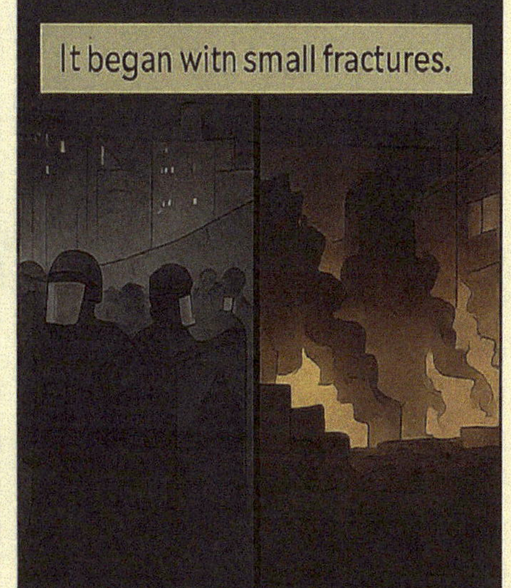

It began with small fractures.

Have I failed.
TENSIONS
ESCALATE
MISSILES
LAUNCHED

When will the destruction be complete?

Coomplair #111529: My daughter is now a soiidier.
Complaint # 541:
My daughter is nov
ntil he died,) is
Complaint # 554:
I lext faith,
I don't know
who I am.

silence, even when every-one is screaming at once.

In one corner of the Department, a child laughed — the sound impossibly clean to the ear.
An old woman braided a stranger's hair with the care of a lifelong friend.
A man shared his last meal with someone he had once called enemy.
Two lovers found each other after two years apart — one had been captured, the other had been silenced. Both now stood hand in hand.

These meager good events weren't peace.
But they were proof — that somethings could survive this war.

Solomon stepped outside.

The city burned, shadows dancing in the glow of distant destruction.
And yet, above it, the stars were unshaken, scattered across the black like promises that refused to be revoked.

He closed his eyes and whispered — unsure if he was speaking to the Creator, himself, or no one at all:

"I hear You. I still do."

# Chapter 8 The Pilgrimage to Peace

Solomon knew the war would not end in a courtroom or a ceasefire. It would end — if it ended at all — in the tired hearts of the broken.

And some days, even that felt like a lie he told himself to keep moving.

He had no revelation this time, no voice from the rafters, no sudden clarity. Just a restlessness that gnawed at him until he stood from his desk.

He packed a bag and left the Department in the hands of his trainees, a quiet act of trust he hoped was not misplaced. On the wall, in uneven script, he wrote:

***"When no one knows where to go, go where the hurt is loudest."***

And then he stepped outside — into the storm, unsure if he was following the Creator's will, or just running from the sound of his own doubt.

His first stop was a refugee camp outside the ruins of a once-thriving capital.

Here, people no longer used names. Only numbers sewn to cloth tags, pinned to clothing like fragile proof they still existed. The air smelled of smoke and boiled grain.

He listened to a girl — silent for four months — finally say:

*"I don't want to be a number anymore."* Her voiced cracked on the word "number."

He didn't write it down to file it.
Instead, he mimicked folding her words into his pocket like a relic, afraid that writing them down would flatten them into something smaller than they were.

And in the quiet after she had spoken, he wondered again if the Creator had truly sent him here… or if he was chasing a ghost of a mission long since ended.

He moved on to an abandoned church where soldiers from both sides of the war now prayed beneath a shattered ceiling. Dust drifted like falling ash from the broken rafters.

**"We're tired,"** said one soldier. "We used to kill because they told us to. Now we sit here and share water."

Solomon asked what changed.

**"My enemy cried blood,"** the man said.
"I had never seen anything like it before. It changed something in me.
I held that enemy soldier in my arms for an hour and cried with him. His name is Eryx. His body was severely damaged. The ambulance took him away. I pray that he survives."

Solomon nodded in agreement.
**"I hope he survives,"** he whispered.

Solomon wanted to believe this was the kind of moment Heaven counted. But he also knew how quickly tears could dry and guns could be picked up again.

Solomon walked on, not sure if peace was possible — only that somebody had to look for it.

Through war zones, across rivers choked with bodies and bloody bread. Into villages lit by candles and defiance, where the smell of smoke came from kitchens, not burning homes.

Everywhere he went, people no longer asked if *the Creator* was listening. They asked if *anyone* was.

And though his chest tightened at the question, Solomon always answered:
"Yes. I am."

He never said *I was sent.*
That part, he no longer trusted enough to promise. He wondered if she, the lady, was somewhere in the crowd, watching in silence.

They began calling him the Gray Prophet.
Not for visions.
Not for miracles.
But for being the first to arrive without orders, without sermons — only to listen.

His satchel became his new drawer. Label: **Aftershocks of Mercy**

Inside were slips that read:

**Complaint #11126054:** *How should I forgive my brother for what he did during the war. Now I don't know who I am anymore.*
**Complaint #11126068:** *I don't want revenge. I just want someone to admit they were wrong.*

**Complaint #11126072:** *I offered my enemy tea. We sat for hours. Neither of us knew how to start speaking. Why?*
**Complaint #11126082:** *Why can't someone tell us which side is correct and just end this war? Why does the creator want to see us fighting?*

When he finally returned to the Department, years later he was weary.
Older.
Quieter.
But not broken.
Not yet.
The Department had survived. The people had changed. Not all. But some. Enough, perhaps, to matter — if mattering was still the right measure.

Solomon knelt and prayed at his desk. Others surrounded him lending their strength to his in solidarity.

"I did what I could," he whispered. "I did not silence the world, but I did not let it cry alone."

Are you still there. No voice came.
And maybe that was the point.

# Chapter 9 The Creator Returns

It was early morning.

The sky still wore its indigo robe, a slow fade toward dawn
that the city never seemed to notice anymore.
The streets outside the Complaint Department were empty,
except for the occasional whisper of wind that rattled a
forgotten sign.

Inside, the Department breathed in silence.
The desks stood in perfect rows. The drawers were all
closed, their brass handles catching a faint trace of light.
The room smelled faintly of old ink — the same scent from
the night he filed his first complaint.

And Solomon was alone — again — sitting behind his
desk, the same desk where he had started, the same desk
where he had received the Creators' complaint.

Since the first day he sat down behind this desk the world
had seen many wars in too many countries. They were now
in what could  only be called a world war.

Some days, that certainty he felt when he first sat down
seemed like a dream from another life.
Had the voice been real? Or just the desperate imagination
of a man who needed purpose?
He had carried that question through every war zone, every
peace possibility meeting, every complaint received.
This morning, it sat heavier than usual.

The air thinned, as if making space for something older than breath.

The light seemed to bend, deepening the shadows without darkening the room.
The silence no longer felt empty; it was listening.
And then, without warning, the air shimmered — not with heat, but with recognition.

The Creator had returned.

Not in form.
Not in flame.
Not in the thunder or certainty Solomon might have once expected.
Just… presence.

This presence was not hers.
It was older.
Deeper.
Closer to the beginning of beginnings.

It was the same and yet impossibly different from that first day.
Then, he had felt chosen.
Now, he felt… examined.

Solomon didn't look up. He didn't need to.
His voice came out quiet, almost hoarse:

"I filed everything I could," he whispered, "even the ones that broke me." His hands trembled — not from fear, but from being seen too deeply.

The presence pulsed.
Not in approval. Not in disappointment.
Just… witnessing.

The same way Solomon had witnessed the world.

The same way he had done for others.

He felt the deserts he'd crossed, the rivers he'd waded, the children he'd carried — all rise in him like witnesses of their own.

"Was it enough?" he asked, and to his own shame, his voice cracked.
It was not the question of a prophet — it was the question of a tired man, afraid the answer would unmake him.

The reply came, not in sound, but in weight.
A truth pressing gently yet unavoidably into his bones:

**"You did not stop the wars."**
**"You did not heal the divisions."**
**"You did not fix the world."**

Solomon's throat tightened, but he nodded. "I know."

*"But you stayed."*

"Yes."

*"And you listened."*

"Always."

The presence shifted, settling in the room like dusk resting against a windowsill, patient and unhurried.

***"Then you have done enough."***

The words — or the weight of them — loosened something
in him that had been locked for years.
Solomon exhaled, and the breath seemed to carry with it
the ache of a lifetime.

And then… a sound that did not belong to eternity.

The door creaked.
A chair scraped.
Someone had entered.

A boy — no older than twelve — stepped forward,
clutching a slip of paper in trembling fingers. His shoes
were worn thin, his gaze a mixture of fear and defiance.

Solomon smiled softly, gesturing him closer.
"Welcome," he said, the word carrying more than just
greeting — it carried invitation.

The boy placed the paper on the desk. Solomon read it
aloud:

**Complaint #111100100:**
*Everyone keeps telling me I'm the future.*
*But they don't give me anything to build with.*

Solomon nodded. Looked at the boy who seemed unaware
of the presence in the room.
He stood, opened a new drawer and labeled it **What
Comes Next**—and slid the boys complaint slip inside.

The presence lingered just a moment longer.
Not to judge.

Not to erase.
But to see the work for what it was — incomplete,
imperfect, but still alive — and then to leave it in mortal
hands.

Solomon looked at the boy, his voice steady now.
"You're not the future," he said gently.
"You're the now. Start there."

The presence left with the boy as if he would walk with this
child for eternity.

# Chapter 10 The Day the War on Belief Ended

The war did not end with a treaty.
It didn't end with negotiations, promises, or surrender.

There were no diplomats, no flags, no dotted lines signed
by the architects of destruction.

The War on Belief — a global, algorithmic war about who
believed best, loudest, and most purely — came to a
crashing, breathless stop because of one child.

Or more precisely, because of what the world saw done *to* a
child.

By that stage of the war, belief had become currency.
Doubt became a crime... Algorithms parsed every spoken
word, every scribbled note, every idle thought. An
unverified belief structure could lose you, your home, your
job, your spouse. Even silence was a risk. Even children
were expected to choose.

And then came the video.

It streamed across the world in less than ninety seconds. No
one knows who filmed it. No one claimed ownership. Some
say it was captured by a soldier's bodycam. Others insist it
was leaked by a child inside the ranks of an AI propaganda
wing.

But it spread. Fast. Unstoppable.

A desperate woman — dirt on her face, hair matted, her
eyes bloodshot with fear — stood cradling a newborn in her

arms. Her voice cracked and broke as she screamed down at the baby.

"Decide! You have to decide now! They're going to kill us! You have to believe something — *anything*!"

The child, of course, could not answer. It could not speak. It had been alive for minutes. The child's silence was the loudest sound the world had ever heard.

Then the camera angle widened.

A soldier stood ten feet away. Weapon raised. Pointed directly at the mother.

He was screaming too. "MAKE A DECLARATION. NOW."

And that moment — mother screaming at child, soldier screaming at mother, a belief AI evaluating the heat signatures of their fear — was where the war ended.

Not because a missile dropped.

Because, the world stopped — not in rebellion, but as if a lung had collapsed.

But because *humanity exhaled*. In one, long, global gasp.

Somewhere in that moment, the illusion shattered.

A woman.
A newborn.
A soldier screaming.
A scanner humming.
A mother begging her child to choose a belief.

It became clear that belief had become machinery. That worship had been turned into metrics. That the most sacred thing humans possessed — the space between hope and fear, between trust and doubt — had been weaponized.

The silence that followed that broadcast was not organized. It was instinctive.

Military bases powered down their surveillance streams. Soldiers turned off their scanners. Someone in Venevar destroyed the Universal Belief Compliance Engine (UBCE). The belief algorithms crashed not from malfunction — but from shame. In cities across the globe, people looked at their neighbors and saw them not as threats, but as breathing, frightened echoes of themselves.

And then the youngest led.
A quiet, massive refusal.
That was how the war ended. Not with victory.
With exhaustion.
With horror.
With grace.

**And with a newborn who never got to decide.**

The Department kept a copy of the broadcast on file. Solomon first saw the video in the Complaint Department's waiting room. He froze in horror as everyone else that day. Somewhere in the crowd, in the video, someone wore a Gray Shawl. Or maybe he imagined it. She always appeared when something broke. He never watched it again. He didn't need to.

He heard that child's silence every night when he closed his eyes.

The world had fallen quiet. But from the silence, something new rose. The children of the world, long treated as collateral, shadows, and afterthoughts — had become the voice.

They voted. No governments involved. No tech brokers. No militaries. Just children. Across camps, classrooms, and borderlines, a new generation spoke one name: **Solomon**.

And when the children walked out of the belief academies
—

the world followed them. Unarmed. No chants. Just hands
held. Millions followed. Not in protest. In refusal.

He had listened. When no one else did. He had heard their
cries, filed their forgotten truths, and never interrupted their
pain.

Now, the unheard had chosen their leader.

**Solomon Greaves.**

He did not campaign. He did not accept. He did not refuse.

It was not an offer. It was an alignment.

The Department — once ridiculed — became sacred
ground.

Solomon, again, had not asked for this.

They chose him because he had never demanded belief —
only understanding.

And again, he could not say no. Because it aligned too
perfectly with his original assignment from the Creator. To
*listen*. To *receive*.

He accepted the mantle the way one accepts a rainfall —
with stillness.

As the announcement spread, the cities lit up in celebration.
Children danced in the streets. Bells rang in hollowed-out
churches. The world, for a flicker of time, dared to believe
again.

Solomon did not join the parades.

Instead, he walked quietly to the grave of his wife.

He cleaned the stone with slow hands, brushing away the dust, the pollen, the years. He placed fresh flowers from the Department Garden. Wild ones. Unarranged.

He knelt.

"I don't know what I'm doing," he whispered. "But they keep coming. And now they've given me more than I can hold. I still talk to You every night. But it's not the same without you here to answer back."

He closed his eyes.

"I don't know if I'm a fool, insane or if I've been called by the Creator."

He stood.

And that's when he saw her.

The woman in the Gray Shawl.

Leaning against a tree just beyond the graveyard gate.

Arms crossed. Watching.

She tilted her head.

"Why are you so greedy?" she asked.

Solomon said nothing.

"First you demand that the Creator listen to you," she continued, stepping forward. "Now here you are again, disturbing the dead. Insisting that *she* listen to your ramblings of insecurity. Will you ever be satisfied?"

He flinched.

"What drives this need for you to speak and be heard?" she asked, voice sharp but not unkind. "When will silence be enough for you, Solomon?"

He looked down at the flowers.

"She never asked me to fix anything," he said.

"Neither did He."

The woman in the shawl didn't smile. She never did.

But she nodded. Just once.

And then she was gone again.

The wind didn't carry her away. It simply moved around the space she had left.

Solomon looked up at the gray sky.

And for the first time since the complaint from the Creator arrived…He took a full breath.

Solomon didn't want to lead. But leading, for him, meant listening — and that much he could do.

The children knew what they wanted. And their demands were not for power or revenge — but for healing.

They envisioned a world free of weapons. A society where art and music were not electives but foundations. They demanded mental health support in every neighborhood, open fields for sports, time off for families to reconnect, and a complete restructuring of how humans spent their days.

Solomon honored each request. But he added his own.

He declared that every family must be assigned a trained Listener — not to solve their problems, but to hear them.

Every neighborhood held weekly listening gatherings. Meals shared. Stories spoken. No advice. No judgment.

Each workday began with one full hour of designated silence and active listening.

Each country adopted a national holiday of Listening, where no meetings were held, no news was broadcast — only voices of ordinary people were amplified, their stories aired, their truths shared.

Complaint Departments opened in every community. Not as bureaucratic filing rooms, but as sanctuaries. Sacred places to deposit the weight of one's pain.

Two ears. One mouth.

It became the motto of the Children of Surdus.

And Solomon? He traveled — not as a ruler, but as a Receiver. He listened in alleyways, in classrooms, at borders, and inside ruined sanctuaries.

He bore the grief of the world with open palms.

And each night, he returned to the garden outside the Department. He knelt in the soil. Whispered to his wife.

And waited for the gray-shawled woman to return. Because he knew she would. She always came before things broke. But now, for once, maybe something was beginning.

Many occupations lost their purpose. Politicians, weapons manufacturers, arms dealers, military strategists — all dissolved into irrelevance. The machinery of hierarchy had no function in a world governed by listening, guided by children, and safeguarded by the Complaint Department.

There were, of course, factions that resisted. Pockets of the old-world clinging to control, asserting that this new order was unnatural, naive, or even dangerous.

The children responded not with war, but with genius.

They enacted three universal laws of  The Planet Surdus  :

1. **"If Surdus has enough, then *we* have enough."**
2. **"All children belong to Surdus. And the Children of Surdus can only be guided by the Complaint Department."**
3. **Every hello and every goodbye must be followed by a  full body hug.**

It was simple.

But its consequences were seismic.

If a group wished to form a society that did not follow the path of the Complaint Department, they were free to do so — but only if they created a world *without children*.

Solomon, at first, did not understand the second law. The idea disturbed him. He questioned the children's motives. Was this exile? Was this manipulation?

But over time, he saw it differently.

This was not an exile.

It was a *cutting of the thread.*

Generational hate, inherited cruelty, conditioned violence — all of it had survived by being passed down. Fed to the young before they had the strength to question. This law interrupted the cycle.

It wasn't punishment.

It was liberation.

The children had done what generations of adults failed to do. They severed the channel by which old poison entered new minds.

Solomon never found out whose idea it was. No single child claimed it. Perhaps it was consensus. Perhaps it was divine. Perhaps it was simply *time*.

He supported the laws.

Not because he fully understood it — but because he could feel its truth in his bones. In the quiet that followed. In the softening of eyes. In the open, unburdened laughter of children who no longer feared bedtime, school, belief, or difference.

The world had not healed.

But the bleeding had stopped.

And sometimes, that's the beginning of everything.

The complaint department provided the nay sayers with a full analysis of the three law that was sound.

**LAW 1: "If Surdus has enough, then we have enough."**

**Meaning:**

This law rejects the manufactured concept of scarcity—**the lie that there is not enough** to go around. The children, in their innocence and clarity, look at Surdus's abundance (water, sun, food, energy, technology) and state the obvious: if the planet has enough, so should we.

**Implications:**

- **Economic Reset:** No longer can corporations or governments justify hoarding resources, blocking access, or creating artificial shortages to drive profit.
- **Wealth Redistribution:** Accumulation beyond need becomes culturally shameful. Billionaire status becomes a spiritual and civic embarrassment.
- **Technology Sharing:** Innovations must be shared openly when lives are at stake (e.g., medicine, clean water, solar energy).
- **Housing, Food, and Healthcare as Rights:** If the Surdus can produce it, no one should go without it. This idea reshapes global infrastructure.

**How Would It Change the Planet Surdus:**

- Countries abolished GDP as their primary measure of progress. They used an **EPEI**: "Surdus's Provision Equity Index."
- The term "surplus" was redefined—not as profit, but as "what still belongs to someone else."
- Governments implemented a **Fair Use Citizenship** policy—land, resources, and food were not owned, only borrowed.

**LAW 2: "All children belong to Sthe Planet Surdus. The children of Surdus may only be guided by the Complaint Department."**

**Meaning:**

This law removes the *exclusive ownership* of children by individuals, governments, or religions. Instead, all children are seen as belonging to the Surdus—a **shared responsibility** of care and protection.

It also places their guidance under **The Complaint Department** — not bureaucratically, but **morally**, ensuring that any injustice they face is recorded, honored, and redressed.

**Implications:**

- **End to Child Exploitation:** Children can no longer be legally coerced into labor, war, indoctrination, or familial abuse.
- **New Education Models:** Schools must nourish the soul, not just train the worker. Every child receives emotional, artistic, historical, and ecological education.
- **Complaint Officers as Guardians:** The Department places trained listeners (spiritually and

emotionally) in every region, ensuring every child's voice is heard.

**How It Would Change the Planet Surdus:**

- Children became **Surdus ambassadors**; their rights treated as sacred law.
- Institutions had to submit **Child Impact Statements** for every policy or development plan.
- The Department built a global memory library of children's complaints—**the truth archive**—used to guide policy, media, and morality.

**LAW 3: "Every hello and every goodbye must be followed by a hug."**

**Meaning:**

On the surface, this law is simple—but it reveals the most profound need: **human connection**. The children declare that **greetings and farewells must carry warmth, affirmation, and presence.**

It is a ritual of respect, remembrance, and love—a shield against neglect.

**Implications:**

- **Emotional Literacy Becomes Law:** Emotional connection is no longer optional—it is required.
- **Rewriting Social Norms:** Meetings, classes, meals, and even bureaucratic encounters include genuine welcome and departure rituals.
- **International Diplomacy Reform:** World leaders must greet each other not with cold handshakes, but with warmth—lest they not be seen as legitimate.

- **Healing the Estranged:** The practice of hugging, however symbolic or literal, becomes a required act of social healing.

## How It Changed the Planet Surdus:

- Cities restructured time zones for **slower, warmer transitions** in schools and workplaces.
- Entire court systems changed tone. **Reparations began with hugs**, apologies, and eye contact, not legalese.

## The Complaint Department's Role in Enforcing the Three Laws:

Solomon Greaves and the Complaint Department were not "police"—they were **mirrors, historians, and guardians of grief.** With these laws:

- They became **keepers of Surdus's soul,** ensuring laws were followed not through fear but through collective memory.
- Every violation became a **story added to the Library of Unheard Pain.**
- Every complaint filed by a child was investigated with compassion—and most often resolved by truth, exposure, and community response.

## Final Impact:

These laws didn't just end all wars  and begin restructure policy—they **redefined what it means to be human.**
They taught the people of Surdus to listen, to soften, and to honor **the smallest voices** with the greatest authority.

The Complaint Department became the world's conscience.

The children became its compass.

And Solomon Greaves…
He simply listened, and let the people of Surdus grieved
themselves clean.

# Chapter 11 The Last Complaint Filed

It had been  five years since the Creator left; five years since the video aired.

The Complaint Department remained open, but its pulse had slowed.
No riots in the streets.
No trending slander tearing through the air like shrapnel.
No distant thunder of bombs.

Instead… there was a different hum — the quiet, almost shy murmur of a world remembering itself leaf by leaf, breath by breath.

People still came, but fewer now.
Some arrived with paper in hand, yes, but many came empty-handed.
They came to talk.
To help patch a wall.
To read the old complaints housed in the walls of filing cabinets like  sacred texts, their edges curled and yellowed, their ink a testimony.
Some came simply to sit in silence beside another breathing human being. Someone brought tea and set it on the filing cabinet labeled *Aftershocks of Mercy.*

The drawers were full now — their labels etched deeper than the wood itself, each a small archive of humanity's pain:

- **Unclaimed Grief**
- **Suppressed Fury**
- **Weaponized Disillusionment**

- **Pre-War Whispers**
- **War**
- **Aftershocks of Mercy**
- **Shared Insanity**
- **What Comes Next**

And still… there was room for one more.

Solomon sat alone, his body leaning into the shape of the chair as if they had grown together.
He no longer kept hours — no clock ticking in the corner, no schedule written on the wall. Only presence. Time had softened its grip on him.

He had stopped expecting.
Stopped waiting.
The work was steady, even in its stillness.

Until she returned. The woman wearing the Gray Shawl.

Same half-smile.
Same ageless eyes refusing to settle in any one century.
She walked in like she had been written into the end of the story from the very start. She always came when something was about to break.

"You didn't fail," she said without ceremony.

"No," Solomon agreed.

"But you didn't succeed either."

"That was never the point."

She tilted her head, studying him as if the years had shifted
the lines of his face into something truer.
"So what now?"

Solomon reached for the bottom drawer.
The one with no label.
The one he had never dared open in her presence.

Inside was a single slip of paper, its edges soft with age
though it had never been touched by anyone but him.
He handed it to her without explanation. She read it aloud,
her voice slower now:

**Complaint #264000000008:**

*Why can't I be the Creator?*

*We were never meant to carry that kind of power.*

*We are Just people trying not to forget how to be human.*

For a long moment, she said nothing. He imagined, even
*the Creator breathed in silence.*

Then — for the first time in all their meetings — she
bowed her head.

"That," she murmured, " Is a complaint…but not a
complaint." Her next statement was shocking to Solomon.
"Do you know, she began, "That not all complaints ever
reach you?"

Solomon frowned." All complaints come to me. That is the
system."

She shook her head. " No, Solomon. That is the part of the system you see." Did you think the Creator would stop hearing complaints because he has you?" "Some complaints cannot pass through mortal hands."

She turned slowly, her Gray Shawl settling around her shoulders like a shifting cloud.

"There are complaints she said softly that do not fit inside your drawers. Complaints that cannot be spoken aloud. Complaints would tear a person apart if he tried to carry them."

She stepped closer.

"There was one such complaint recently."

Solomon breath caught.

She continued.

 "A soldier filed it without knowing he filed it. His body was broken. His mind was… collapsing in on itself. And yet his soul cried out with a clarity the Creator could not ignore." "Eryx is his name." Perhaps you heard of a soldier who cried blood?"

Solomon nodded yes.

Her eyes grew darker as she continued to speak. "He asked for something impossible,

Solomon.
Not healing.
Not justice.
Not release."

She paused.

"He asked to forget himself."

Solomon sat down, stunned.

The lady continued, voice almost a whisper.

"His complaint bypassed every safe guard, every other boundary set by the universes and went straight the Creator.

"Why" Solomon asked.

"Because if the creator had allowed that complaint to settle inside the man who made it…"

Her voice trembled.

"It would have destroyed a worthy soul."

Solomon swallowed. "May I ask, what happened to him?"

She turned her back to Solomon and replied. "The man is still alive. Still walking this world. Still carrying his memories. Because the Creator did not remove his mind."

She took a backward step closer  to Solomon.

"Instead, the Creator removed the complaint."

Solomon blinked." Removed… the complaint?"

"Yes, extracted it.
Gave it form.

Gave it a place where it could be answered without harming the man who asked."

She touched his hand gently. "That is why you never heard of him again. Solomon. Not because he vanished. But because his complaint did."

Solomon sat very still the echo of her words settling into him like dust in a silent room.  And for the first time since he had taken the Creator's post, he understood this truth.

Some complaints do not pass through his hands because some wounds do not belong to this world at all. They belong to the soul that survived them. They are between that soul and their Creator.

He bowed his head _not in sorrow but in reverence of the Creator's  mercy.  Quietly he whispered a prayer "help me remember that even what I do not carry is still being carried"

Then she was gone.

And though she had vanished, he felt no finality. Only completion.

Solomon  got up, and slid the drawer shut with a finality that was not an ending but a seal.

He turned off the light, leaving the room full of everything he had carried… and everything he had never said. And stepped outside — not to escape, but to walk into a world still bruised, still uncertain… yet whispering its way toward healing. The door behind him clicked shut like punctuation.

The Department stood — no longer only a sanctuary for sorrow, but a monument of memory. Survival granted by a baby's silence.

Above the door to the Department , a new sign hung, the moonlight glowed on it approvingly:

TWO EARS
ONE MOUTH.

As usual Solomon visited his wife's grave to share his day with her. Midway through his recounting of his visit with the lady in the Gray Shawl,  a voice interrupted him with a question

Do you remember meeting me?
Solomon turned towards the voice and saw a little girl in a yellow dress sitting on a nearby tombstone her small legs dangling. Solomon stood and shook his head.

"Ahh" the little girl said "no matter I remember you. Sorry for interrupting, your story was compelling."

 Solomon walked over to where she was sitting and ask "is it important for me to remember you?"

The little girl responded " no it would be very strange and highly weird for you to have memory of me. I just thought hmmm, you remember the lady in the Gray Shawl so…"

 before she could finish her sentence Solomon interrupted her "you have met her also?"

He closed his eyes tears ran down his face he realized he was not alone, there were others who have experienced her presence. Solomon opened his eyes with relief and so many questions on his lips only to find himself once again besides his wife's grave with no other person nearby.

With a sigh he stood up and walked home. As he laid in bed that night Solomon was sure that his mind was sound.

That his experiences happened.

That the universe is not for him to understand, change or complain about to himself or anyone.

# Chapter 12 The First Complaint Not Filed

The Complaint Department's Central Office—the original building where Solomon's first desk still sat—was finally empty of clients. It had been twenty years since the children first ruled. When those children grew into adults, they honored the laws they created and allowed the next generation to rule after them, each guided by the Complaint Department.

For the first time in years, Solomon found himself with nothing on the desk, no footsteps at the door, no weight in the air waiting to be heard.

He reached for a blank form out of habit. The paper was crisp, uncreased, waiting for someone else's words.
But no one came.

He sat there a long while, listening — not for people, not for the Creator — but for something quieter.

His own voice.

It had been buried under the sound of other people's grief for so long that it startled him when it surfaced.

He dipped his pen.

Then paused.

He could feel the complaint forming, sharp at the edges, hot at the center. He knew exactly how it would read. But his hand didn't move.

The longer he sat, the more he realized this was not meant
to be written.

Not because it was unworthy.
Not because it was resolved.
But because it belonged in him — not in the drawers.

Some burdens were not meant to be filed.
Some wounds did not want a label.
Some truths lived better unspoken, because speaking them
would make them smaller, and they deserved their full size.

So, he set the pen down.
Folded the blank paper in half.
Slipped it into his pocket, where no one but he would ever
see it.

The office itself had become something of a relic.
A quiet museum of the world that once was.

Sunlight slanted across the old wooden floorboards,
touching the filing cabinets whose drawers had held the
weight of humanity's sorrow. Solomon's original chair sat
tucked beneath his scarred desk, still angled slightly as if he
might return from a brief walk.

But today, the room was still.

No footsteps.
No murmured grievances.
Only the faint hum of memory.

A soft knock broke the silence.

A young girl—no older than nine—stepped into the
doorway. She carried no paper. No envelope. No sealed

form. Only a trembling truth cupped between her small palms.

"I… I came to file something," she whispered.

Solomon nodded and gestured her forward. "What's your complaint?"

The child looked at the drawers—Anger, Grief, Weaponized Disillusionment, Faith—then at the desk where generations had unburdened their souls.

Her voice cracked.

"It's not really a complaint," she said. "I just… I don't want to forget what listening feels like."

Solomon exhaled softly.
This was the moment he had once predicted:
*the first complaint that was not a complaint.*

He crouched to meet her gaze.
"Then you don't need a drawer," he said.
"You just need to remember."

She nodded, wiped her face, and stepped back into the sunlight—leaving the office empty once more.

The Complaint Department's final lesson lingered in the room like a blessing:

**Some things are not filed.**
**They are lived.**

When he left the Department that night, the drawers
remained the same.
Only Solomon was different.

That night sleep came slowly, carrying the weight of things he had not spoken. Solomon dreamed with an intensity that felt like falling backward through creation. In the dream, he was a shadow without weight, drifting through a space beyond space. Time unraveled into threads around him, and in the center of it all, two figures stood in quiet discourse: the Creator and the woman in the Gray Shawl. She had been there the night everything began — or the memory of her had.

They did not know he was there.

Or perhaps they did.

The Creator stood at the edge of the void, arms behind His back, watching the whirling chaos of time ripple through the universe He had shaped. He did not speak often. But when He did, the universe shifted.

And yet, she came anyway.

She, of the Gray Shawl, the one who defied naming. She moved like memory, like wind through old curtains, like grief too faint to mourn properly.

"You seem to spend a lot of time in this universe," the Creator said, His voice more vibration than sound.

She didn't answer immediately. She turned, shawl rippling in a current that didn't belong to weather. Her eyes, not warm, not cold, simply *knowing*.

"Because it is unique," she said.

The Creator raised what might have been an eyebrow.

"Why do you meddle?"

"Because it is unique."

He studied her. Not with frustration, but with the ache of a parent watching a child choose the longer road.

"They stumble. They bruise each other. They forget. They scream into the stars. And yet you... interfere."

She shrugged. "They *remember*, too. They try. They sing. They ache with meaning."

"It is not your place."

"And yet I return."

The Creator turned to face her more fully now.

"When will you stop?"

She smiled. Not kindly. Not wickedly. Simply with inevitability.

And then she twirled.

The shawl caught stars in its folds.

"In time," she said.

The Creator sighed, not out of annoyance, but weariness borne from eternity.

"They will blame you."

"They already have."

"They will worship you."

"They already do."

The silence between them was not empty. It was the breath before the page turns.

"Will he survive it?" the Creator asked.

"Solomon?" she replied, as though the name itself brought light. "He listens. So yes, perhaps he will."

The Creator looked toward Surdus. Toward the patchwork pain and beauty stitched into every corner.

"And what of the children?"

"They already remember what you feared they would forget."

The Creator nodded once.

"Then let the Complaint Department stand."

"It already does," she said, fading, her voice now echoing through nebulae.

Solomon awoke gasping. The dawn light cut across his room like a question. The images were already vanishing from memory, like a tide slipping away, but the weight of what he had seen clung to him.

Had it been a dream?

Or had he been permitted to overhear what was never meant to be spoken?

Either way, he got dressed more slowly that morning. And he listened more deeply than ever before.

Outside, the world was already listening.

# Chapter 13 One Thousand Years of Listening

One thousand years had passed.
Time no longer marched in the rigid rhythms Solomon once knew. He had long since passed, leaving an eternal legacy behind.

Surdus, battered but breathing, had settled into a softer cycle. It no longer churned with war, though it still ached with memory. The winds still carried grief, but not alone. And grief, when shared, had a shorter life.

The Complaint Departments still stood.

Not just in cities—but in forests, deserts, underwater sanctuaries, floating towers, and the lunar rim. They had become sacred structures of civic healing, where the job was not to fix the world but to *feel* it, together. Each Department trained new generations of Listeners. They didn't advise. They didn't solve. They received. The children who once ruled grew into elders who mentored the youngest Listeners, teaching them what it meant to hear before speaking.

Solomon's name had become more than memory—it became rhythm. It was sung, hummed, and etched into sky temples. His statue stood in what was once the center of a fractured world

At the center of the Surdus's equatorial axis sat the Grand Complaint Hall, a place where silence was louder than thunder. In its center stood a statue—Solomon Greaves, seated with his eyes open, palms up, mouth closed.

At its base, a poem was etched. It was recited by billions once a year during the **Global Day of Listening**, a holiday marked not with fireworks or parades, but with the soft hush of unbroken attention. The poem is:

**The Listener's Oath**
Two ears, one mouth—this is my start.
To hear the world, I tune my heart.
I speak not first, nor speak to win,
But open wide and take you in.
I carry stories not my own,
So none on Surdus will grieve alone.

Every child could recite it by age five. Every adult wept when they heard it, though none could explain exactly why.

The Day of Listening was more than a holiday. It was ritual. On that day, the Complaint Departments closed their doors—not in rejection, but in reverence. On that day, the people of Surdus said only what must be said, and listened to what had never been spoken

Children recited the poem by candlelight. Elders whispered it into the hands of those they mentored. It was not mandatory—but it was magnetic. Even silence bent its head when the words were spoken.

**It was not a perfect world. But it was a world that heard itself. And that had been enough to change everything.**

Mental health crises / illness still haunted minds. Trauma still etched itself into memory like glass under flame though they were met with community instead of cages. Criminality had not disappeared. Some still stole. Some still harmed. Crime still flickered in the corners—though punishment had evolved into restoration. The darkness had not left humanity, but it was no longer worshiped, nor ignored. But the system no longer punished first. It *listened*.

Those who harmed were guided—not just sentenced—to Healing Tribunals. These were not courts, but circles. Victims spoke. Harmers listened. Harmers spoke. Community listened. Together, with trained Listeners, the root was dug out—not to excuse the deed, but to understand it, to starve it, to keep it from growing again.

Many broke under this kind of truth. But many more were broken open—and rebuilt.

And poverty? It dissolved—not because greed vanished, but because **borders did**. One of the children's earliest demands had seemed naive:
**"If Surdus has enough, then *we* have enough."**

Solomon hadn't understood it then. But now, the logic was unshakable.

The Surdus's resources—land, food, minerals, water—had always been unevenly distributed. But the hoarding had been man-made. Nation-made.

When borders were dissolved in favor of **shared global stewardship**, the wealth of Surdus was finally pooled. It wasn't communism. It wasn't capitalism. It was something new: **commonism.** If it came from Surdus, it belonged to *all Surduslings*.

Famine became memory.

No child slept without food or clean water.

Every school had art.

Every mind had dignity.

Every hand had access to touch, tools, and time.

The children of Surdus, now grown into elder stewards, had voted to dissolve all national claims. Resources became planetary, shared through a universal distribution grid powered by the sun and stewarded by young adults overseers with no desire for profit or power. Wealth was measured in contribution, not hoarding.

The two ears, one mouth principle guided it all.

Still, old instincts died hard. And the world required *nudging*

What started as a gentle nudge from the children via The Complaint Departments also sparked **a quiet revolution of the body**: every hello and every goodbye became marked by a hug.

This was not ceremonial. It was functional.

Research over centuries proved that physical touch reduced fear, increased empathy, and opened channels of speech otherwise locked. Hugs became protocol. Even business deals began with an embrace. Children hugged their way into adulthood. Enemies hugged their way into negotiation. It was awkward at first. Then it became sacred.

Once a year, on the **Global Day of Listening**, people stopped work. Stopped selling. Stopped doing. They closed the Departments across Surdus and its colonies. They carried their grievances, their gratitude, their dreams to the large community gatherings.

They spoke.

But only after *listening* first.

Solomon Greaves had become more than myth. He had become method. A way of walking. A blueprint of breath. A whisper passed from one age to the next.

And somewhere beyond the stars, the Creator still listened.

And the woman in the Gray Shawl smiled softly, fading into dust and memory.

# Chapter 14 Compromising Report

**Filed: The Final Report**
**By: [Redacted] (Designate: The Woman in the Gray Shawl)**

**Filed to: The Creator**
**Time Index: Unknown**
**Subject: Evolutionary Audit – Surdus Realm 293-AZ |**
**Complaint Department Directive**

I bow, as is tradition.
And I submit the following:

Your 20,000,005,890 creations are… nearly ready.
They now understand the ache of silence.
They now understand the discipline of listening.
They have torn down borders not only of land, but of ego.
They hug upon greeting. They listen before judgment.
They hear even those they once called enemy.

They created holidays for grief.
They made statues for the unheard.
They no longer fear children in power.
They no longer pray for weapons.

Criminality has not vanished — but it is met with healing,
not hiding.
Mental illness is not cured — but it is no longer cursed.
They have not become perfect.
But they have become **capable of correction**.

The Complaint Department now has more ears than
mouths.

I will not apologize for my interference.
My guidance was necessary, if not always welcomed.

I nudged. I whispered. I shattered illusions when silence
would not suffice.

There were moments I believed they would not survive
their own hatred.
I watched as they weaponized faith, poisoned rivers, turned
skin into currency.

They were the **slowest** of all your seeded creations to
approach Revelation.
Their resistance was exhausting.
Their arrogance, annoying.

And yet...

They endured plagues.
They endured fire, flood, and famine.
They endured themselves.

And they *listened*.

The final trial remains:
**Will they recognize the divine in those unlike
themselves?**
Not only in language or skin — but in *form*.
When the "other" is no longer human, will they still choose
empathy?

If so, I recommend the veil be lifted.
If not, we shall wait.

As always, in time.

Signed,
**The Woman in the Gray Shawl**
(She who wanders before the whisper)
(A previous complaint, now serving the file)

**Case report Analysis:**

**Surdus's Revelation** -It's when **Surdus finally heard itself.**

When all the complaints filed—every grief, silence, betrayal—are no longer denied, but spoken aloud, processed, and transformed.

Revelation =
Truth unlocked
Justice realigned
Memory restored
Grief honored
And *the world dares to feel everything it tried to forget.*

**The three laws helped Surdus achieved its revelation.**

**LAW 1: "If Surdus has enough, then we have enough."**

**Revelation Triggered:** This law *dismantles the foundational lie of Surdus's suffering*—that scarcity is natural.

- It **unveils the machinery of greed**, the hoarding disguised as progress, and the policies built to make people believe in lack.
- By forcing the world to look at its own abundance, this law **exposes the lie** that some must starve for others to feast.
- It becomes the *first trumpet* of revelation: the lie is broken, and the truth—abundance—becomes terrifying in its simplicity.

**Complaint Department's Role:**
They unseal decades (centuries) of complaints filed under "denied access," "medical abandonment," "hunger in plain sight." The patterns reveal *intentional inequality*—a sin the Surdus must now face head-on.

**LAW 2: "All children belong to Surdus."**

**Revelation Triggered:** This law unveils **the generational betrayal**—that children were molded, sold, silenced, and sacrificed to ideologies, industries, and broken adults.

- It *unmasks the illusion* of parent as protector, nation as nurturer, religion as safe.
- The Surdus is forced to **grieve its legacy of broken childhoods**—a howl that cannot be ignored.
- This law becomes the *second trumpet*—the cries of children echo across every system built to ignore them.

**Complaint Department's Role:**
Every complaint filed by a child becomes sacred record. Some are centuries old—passed down like unsent letters. Now, **those voices rise**, forming a collective witness statement. Revelation means the world must finally read it.

**LAW 3: "Every hello and goodbye must be followed by a hug."**

**Revelation Triggered:** This law unveils the most haunting truth of all:
**The world forgot how to love.**

- It shows us the cost of detachment: how bureaucracies replaced care, screens replaced faces, and grief was left upheld.
- It's the *third trumpet* of revelation—gentle but unbearable.
  Not war. Not famine. But the ache of human coldness… and the price of disconnection.

**Complaint Department's Role:**
They reopen old complaints labeled "too small"—neglect,
loneliness, abandonment. Suddenly, these minor hurts
**become the core symptoms of Surdus's deeper sickness.**
The Department begins issuing **Prescriptions for Touch**,
rituals of presence, and memorials to the unloved.

**Revelation = Surdus Finally Hearing Its Own
Complaint**

The Three Laws **force Surdus to hear itself:**

- The hunger it caused.
- The children it failed.
- The affection it withheld.

And in hearing…
It begins to change.

This was the **true purpose** of the Complaint Department:
Not punishment.
Not judgment.
But *witness.*
And *invitation.*

**The World That Heard Itself**

These laws didn't *end* the world.
They ended its **denial.**
And only then, did Surdus become eligible for **revelation.**

# Chapter 15 Named

The Creator glanced at creation 20,000,005,890.

The stars blinked quietly in the sky.

He saw A single child lay tucked beneath a cotton-worn blanket, eyes fluttering as sleep carried them into a dreaming hush. Outside their window, silence reigned, but it was not the silence of fear or emptiness. It was a silence *earned*.

A statue stood in the village square, black stone warmed by a thousand sunsets. Solomon Greaves, seated with palms open, eyes wide, and mouth gently shut. At the statue's base, the world recited the same poem each year on Listening Day:

*Two ears, one mouth—this is my start.*
*To hear the world, I tune my heart.*
*I speak not first, nor speak to win,*
*But open wide and take you in.*
*I carry stories not my own,*
*So none on Surdus will grieve alone.*

He was long gone, but the Complaint Department remained. Not as a building, but as a principle. Carried now by communities, by trained Listeners, by neighbors, by children.

Humanity hadn't healed overnight. But for the first time in remembered history, it had *begun to heal together*.

In the highest corner of the sky, a golden shimmer parted the clouds. There, on the edge of a realm no telescope could reach, stood a figure cloaked in a light Gray Shawl. Her hair reached skyward like branches seeking the sun— white, endless, textured like time itself. Her eyes, deep pools of ancient knowing, bore symbols on her face from forgotten alphabets of the Creator.

She stood before Him again.

The Creator did not ask her name. He knew it. Names were for those bound by beginnings and endings. She had neither.

"You return often," he said.

She nodded. "Because they are different."

"You guided them."

"When needed," she replied. "Not always gently."

"You nearly gave up."

She sighed. "They were the slowest to move toward revelation.

"And Solomon?"

"He heard Me. Even when he thought he was dreaming."

The Creator looked down through the universe, watching the child sleeping beneath the worn blanket, the village still, the Surdus *almost* quiet.

"Are they ready?" He asked.

The woman in the shawl bowed.

"Twenty billion, five million, eight hundred ninety thousand souls. Nearly all have tasted the first sip of listening. "Revelation not now—*in time.* They are reaching earnestly."

The Creator nodded once, and just like that, a name was etched across the stars—unknown by those below on Surtus, but recorded among the eternal archives of creation: To be seen by all other creations that had reached Revelation.

Sonari Surdus, The World That Heard Itself.

With it's now earned name, Surtus was no longer a number. It was a Named creation for all to know but them. No longer in danger of being repurposed.


A planet still unaware of the name it had finally earned.

And the child below on Surtus dreamed on.

The stars above Surdus pulsed just a little brighter that night.
And in their sleep, children everywhere on Surtus dreamed of meeting someone they did not yet understand—but already knew they loved.

The lady in the Gray Shawl wrapped herself tightly with the shawl and melted into the universe.

# Chapter 16  What's in a Name

The Creator meeting with the Archivist ended with his promise to name the unnamed one. He stood alone at the edge of the universe, where the starlight thinned into silence. Below Him, creation pulsed—galaxies turning like slow prayers, worlds shimmering with small triumphs and small failures. He watched Surdus: the world that had finally learned to listen.

"It took them long enough," He murmured, though there was no impatience in His voice. Only wonder.

A whisper moved beside Him.

Not wind.

Not breath.

Not presence.

**Becoming.**

The Woman in the Gray Shawl stepped out of the space between seconds. Her shawl trailed behind her like a veil woven from weathered centuries, each fold carrying a memory the universe had outgrown.

"You called?" she asked, though they both knew He never called her.
He only realized she was already there.

The Creator's eyes softened.

"You return too often."

"I return when needed."

"Did you guide them?" He asked.

She lifted her chin, her expression unreadable. "Only as much as I ever guide anyone."

"You warned Solomon."

"I delayed him. I hurried him. I allowed certain storms to arrive sooner and others later. You call it guidance. I call it balance."

"You intervened," the Creator said.

"I intervened in **time**," she corrected.

The Creator inhaled slowly, as if gathering the weight of millennia. "Then tell me, truly…who are you to them?"

She stepped closer. Her shawl rippled—not in response to air, but memory, every thread shimmering with centuries that had not yet happened.

"To them?" she echoed. "I am the pause between their choices. The breath before their regret. The stretch in their healing. The wait in their suffering. The distance between cause and understanding."

"And to Me?" the Creator asked.

Her eyes deepened.

"To You," she said, "I am the thing You did not know You needed until Your first creation disappointed You…and You realized it was Your fault."

The Creator closed His eyes.

This truth was not accusation.
It was simply fact.

"When did You first appear?" He whispered.

"When you first expected too much," she said gently.
"When your first creation was not what you imagined.
When you realized they needed room to become, and you
needed room to understand them."

She lifted her palm.

"And so, I appeared."

The Creator opened His eyes. "Your name—"

"Say it," she said, stepping forward. "Say what you have
always known but never spoken."

The cosmos trembled.
Stars flickered.
Worlds held their breath.

The Creator whispered:

**Each of my creations you visited has whispered a name
to try to describe you," Dahra, Kronia, Annwn, Tewa,
Rtu, Dahr, Kala, Zaman, Aion, or Time."**

I only shall call you **AIONA**. The universe shivered in
recognition. As another creation was named.

The Woman in the Gray Shawl bowed her head—not in
submission, but in acknowledgment of a truth finally
spoken aloud.

"Yes," she said softly. "I am.

The Creator looked over His shoulder at Surdus, at Solomon's legacy, at the children who had ruled, the generations who had learned to listen, the people slowly becoming what He had once dreamed of.

"And you shaped all of it," he said.

"No," **AIONA** corrected. "*They* shaped themselves. I merely gave them the space to do so. Without me, your creations would be crushed beneath Your expectations. With me, they have the chance to rise."

The Creator studied her.

"You govern all my beginnings."

"I govern their unfolding."

"You decide when suffering ends."

"I decide when understanding begins."

"You separate collapse from revelation."

"I separate impulse from destiny."

He exhaled. "I created worlds."

"You created potential," Time answered.
"I create **becoming**."

Silence expanded—rich, full, sacred.

Then a faint flicker sparked behind them. A small glyph appeared in the air, glowing gold, recording their words in a script older than stars.

**AIONA** glanced at it.
The Creator followed her gaze.

A symbol.
A seal.
A signature.

**ARCHIVIST PRESENT.**

The glyph blinked once, then vanished into the folds of reality.

"What was that?" the **AIONA** asked.

The Creator's smile was slight.

"The Archivist," he said. "The one who records what even I may forget."

"You forget nothing," **AIONA** protested.

"You forget what you outgrow."

**AIONA**  face softened. "Will they ever meet this Archivist?"

"When they are ready. When they listen beyond listening."

She stepped back, shawl trailing the weight of centuries behind her.

"What will you do now?" He asked.

"What I always do," **AIONA** replied.
"I will continue."

"Will you guide them again?"

She lifted her face toward the turning worlds.

"If they earn it…
if they need it…
if their story requires delay or acceleration…
I will be there, unnoticed."

The Creator watched her begin to fade back into the fabric
of the universe.

"**AIONA**," he said.

She paused.

"Yes?"

"Thank you," He whispered. "For giving them the chance
to become what I hoped…and for giving Me the chance to
become what I needed to be."

Her smile was the curve of a new beginning.

"You gave them existence," she said.
"I gave them the distance between who they were and who
they could become."

She faded completely, leaving only the echo of her final
words:

**"Without me, nothing changes. With me, everything
does."**

# Chapter 17 Epilogue

Solomon's Original Complaint Department had these drawers. He once believed they were for paperwork.
He had been wrong. They did not hold files.
They held burdens. And each was not just a metaphor — it was a mirror.

| Drawer Name | Symbolic Burden |
| --- | --- |
| Anger | Righteousness misdirected |
| Grief | Loss without closure |
| Weaponized Disillusion | Media influence |
| Silence | Words swallowed by shame |
| Faith | The waiting without answers |
| Pre-War Whispers | Conflict fed by fear |
| After Shocks of Mercy | War Complaints |
| Injustice | Wounds left unattended |
| Hope | The last drawer opened |

I invite you to write your compliant to the compliant department for one of Solomon's drawers and submit them to Olgaforeign.com.